Freeman Edwin Miller

Oklahoma, and other Poems

Freeman Edwin Miller

Oklahoma, and other Poems

ISBN/EAN: 9783743303454

Manufactured in Europe, USA, Canada, Australia, Japa

Cover: Foto ©Andreas Hilbeck / pixelio.de

Manufactured and distributed by brebook publishing software
(www.brebook.com)

Freeman Edwin Miller

Oklahoma, and other Poems

Freeman E. Miller.

OKLAHOMA

AND

OTHER POEMS

BY

FREEMAN E. MILLER, A. M.,

PROFESSOR OF ENGLISH LANGUAGE AND LITERATURE IN THE
AGRICULTURAL AND MECHANICAL COLLEGE OF
OKLAHOMA TERRITORY.

BUFFALO
CHARLES WELLS MOULTON
1895

Printed by
CHARLES WELLS MOULTON,
Buffalo, N. Y.

To ope each cage where a heartless age
  Hath chained the birds of singing,
Till Love's own glee that is fond and free
  Shall laugh where they are winging,—
Such is my wish.   'Tis true, hold I,
That songs, like birds, in bondage die.

CONTENTS.

Contents. vii

OKLAHOMA.

OKLAHOMA! Oklahoma!
  Land, O, land of the Fair God,
  Land where ancient, savage races
Through barbarian ages trod!
  Through thy story fancy traces
Facts above what fictions say,
  Where the world with haste advances,—
Born are nations in a day!
  Where the wigwam stood so lonely,
Lordly cities rise in might;
  Where spread desert wildness only,
Fertile farms and homes delight.
  Thou hast summoned to thy bosom
From the ends of all the earth,
  All the youngest, strongest, bravest,
Full of will and wondrous worth.
  O'er thy valleys grow the blossoms
Culled from earth's remotest sod;
  Oklahoma! Oklahoma!
Land, O, Land of the Fair God!

  Oklahoma! Oklahoma!
There is music in thy name,
  There is gladness in thy glory,
There is fondness in thy fame!

In the wonders of thy story
Shines the sheen of noble deed,
　Brighter than the glare of battle
Where the warriors toil and bleed;
　Ruling with immortal forces,
There is found the king of might,
　Over all thy great resources
By the strength of truth and right.
　With thy happy sons and daughters,
Live the virtues fair and pure,
　And the better angels guiding
Keep their hearts and souls secure.
　There are treasures in thy valleys,
There are treasures in thy hills;
　Oklahoma! Oklahoma!
How thy name my bosom thrills!

　Oklahoma! Oklahoma!
Child of law and liberty,
　Thou art always true and tender,
Thou art ever dear to me!
　I will always praises render
To the grandeur of thy worth,
　For the fortunes all presided
At the moment of thy birth.
　Pleasures in their pure completeness
O'er thy pleasant prairies shine,
　And the raptures run with fleetness
Through the happy vales of thine.

Thou art empress of the angels,
Thou art queen of all the gods,
　And the happiness of heaven
O'er thy laughing valleys nods.
　I will always crown with praises
All thy glories, O, my state;
　Oklahoma !　Oklahoma !
Thou art greatest of the great !

　Oklahoma !　Oklahoma !
Bravest are thy noble sons,
　In the thunders of the battle,
And the roaring of the guns !
　Flash of sword and musket's rattle
Never fearful terror gave
　To the staunch and valiant bosoms
Of thy happy hosts and brave.
　When the roars of hell grow louder,
And the mountains shake in fright,
　In the lurid clouds of powder,
They are foremost in the fight;
　And when bayonet and musket,
Sword and saber, slaughter cease,
　They are tenderest and truest
In the silent ways of peace.
　O, my state !　A stream of greatness
From thy mighty people runs;
　Oklahoma !　Oklahoma !
Bravest are thy noble sons !

Oklahoma !   Oklahoma !
Fairest are thy daughters fair,
    In the thousand deeds of duty
Thou hast given them to bear;
    Peerless is their wondrous beauty,
Bright with blushes as the rose,
    Pure as petals of the lily,
White as newly-fallen snows;
    And their voices bright with blessing
Banish misery and woe,
    While their fingers' soft caressing
Soothes the fevers from the brow.
    Souls are always blessed with brightness
Bosoms filled with goodly pearls,
    Hearts forever harvest gladness,
In the glances of thy girls.
    They are robed in golden garments,
Nature's vestments, rich and rare;
    Oklahoma !   Oklahoma !
Fairest are thy daughters fair !

Oklahoma !   Oklahoma !
Sweetest are thy happy homes,
    Smiling in the holy gladness
Which above thee always roams;
    They are never linked with sadness,
They are never bound with pains,
    For the sunshine of enjoyment
Rules the people of thy plains.

Songs are singing with thy maidens,
Music echoes with thy wives,
　　Rapture slays the grief that ladens
All the gladness of their lives.
　　Happiness is with thy husbands,
And thy swains are blest with joy,
　　While the fondest rapture rises
In the hearts of girl and boy.
　　Pleasures linger in thy woodlands,
Gladness on thy prairies roams;
　　Oklahoma! Oklahoma!
Sweetest are thy happy homes!

　　Oklahoma! Oklahoma!
Thou shalt ever live in song;
　　Freedom, near to nature, raises
Temples that to thee belong;
　　Minstrels shall in merry praises
Wind their music o'er thy name
　　Till the voices of the ages
Shout for thee in wild acclaim;
　　They shall sing with tender pleasure
Beauty of thy daughters true;
　　Sing, in high, exultant measure,
Deeds thy sons in battle do.
　　Sages shall in wisdom offer
Full rewards of love to thee,
　　And shall crown thy land and people
Favorites of liberty.

All thy glory shall be shining
Through the cycles clear and strong;
  Oklahoma ! Oklahoma !
Thou : shalt ever live in song !

  Oklahoma! Oklahoma!
Romance of the ages, thou!
    Now, unknown; a moment later,
Kingly crowns upon thy brow!
    Child of all the nations, greater
Shall thy splendors year by year
    Grow unfading, bringing bounties
Full of happiness and cheer!
    Morning saw a desert sleeping,
Worn and wasted with distress;
    Night beheld an empire keeping
Watch above the wilderness.
    Progress with her wand of magic
Touched the sleeping valleys bright,
    And they leaped with instant vigor,
Shaking out their locks of might;
    Earth shall send her fairest blossoms
As a garland for thy brow;
  Oklahoma! Oklahoma!
Romance of the ages thou!

THE RACE FOR HOMES.

APRIL 22, 1889.

BEHOLD! As from the shades of night,
An army gathers full of might,
And strong with constant courage stands
'Tween civilized and savage lands,
Where, vast in power, the legion waits
The turning of the desert gates,
That men of might may enter in
And progress all her glories win!
Lo, where these thousands make assail,
The barren ages all shall fail,
And swift advancement far be hurled,
O'er sleeping empires and the world!

The morning hours haste hurried by;
Behold!   The noon is drawing nigh!
The anxious host with careful eyes
Marks well each rapid hour that flies,
While hope, exulting, wildly rolls
The highest, such as filled the souls
Of Jason and his comrades bold,
Who sought the famous fleece of gold.
Upon the trampled grasses beat
Impatient steeds with restless feet;

The dins of harsh, discordant cries
Above the thrilling thousands rise;
Shrilly the scattered children call,
And soft the words of women fall,
While men with voices hushed and weak
Their low commands expectant speak;
Till suddenly a mighty cry,
A shout of warning, smites the sky:

" Attention!   Ho,
Attention here!
Attention!   Lo,
The noon is near! "
O'er hill and brake
Resounds the warning cry;
The moment great is nigh;
The hosts awake;
Awake, to strive with mad delight,
Awake to win the friendly fight;
And from the camps anear and far,
Where nervous haste and hurry are,
Vast legions gather on the plain,
While chaos and confusion reign;
The neighing steed with quickened pace
Impatient seeks the vantage place;
The slower ox with lightened load
Stands waiting in the crowded road.
And wagon, buggy, carriage, cart,

Vehicles formed with rudest art,
All forward, forward, forward dart,
Swift-forming on the level ground
Where most advantage may be found.

"Line up!   Ho, there,
Line up, line up!"
The hurried order smites the air;
Above the silent prairies fair
Unseen progression holds her cup,
Filled to the brim with magic seeds
That harvests hold for human needs.
Excitement grows on beasts and men;
The saddle girths are tightened o'er,
The stirrups lengthened out once more,
And silence softly falls again;
Each bit and buckle, strap and band,
Is tested o'er with careful hand,
And man and beast in chosen place
Stand ready for the coming race;

The circling sun
His morning race has fully run;
A waving hand
Signals above the brief command
That sight and sense will understand,—
And open swings the desert land!
A shot!   A hundred, thousand more
The grassy meadows echo o'er;

A shout!   From countless throats a shout,
On rolling wings leaps madly out;
A yell, a raging roar, that flies
On bounding winds o'er hill and glen,
And 'round the land electrifies
A thousand living miles of men!
        A mammoth stir,
            A sudden dash,
        Swift whip and spur
            Together clash,
And wheels on wheels that totter crash!
        They're off!   They're off!
        Away, away,
        In mad array!
        No stop nor stay!
The hurried charge they ride to-day
        Would shame and scoff
The Tartar, Turk and Romanoff!
        The race is on;
        The host is gone;
The thronging legions madly ride
        O'er hill and dale,
With hurried pace unsatisfied,
        In fierce assail
        Where none may fail;
And only phantoms dimly blent
Tell where the mounted armies went,
Like shifting shadows, faint and dim,
Or ghostly spectors, gaunt and grim,
Beyond the far horizon's rim!

Behold!   Adown the valleys bright,
The last, lone straggler fades from sight,
And only hasty hoof-beats say
What thousands rode the race to-day;
What hosts, with hearts that build and bless,
Found homes amid the wilderness!

AT PERRY, SEPTEMBER 16, 1893,

CROWDS! Crowds! Crowds!
    Suddenly here as if come from the clouds
        That faded away as they came;
Mad acres of people aflame
With thirst for a morsel of land;
    Wild hunters of fortune, whose game
Is ever escaping the hand;
    Vast, countless, uncountable throngs
With restless, unrestable feet,
    That hurry the ways, full of agonized wrongs,
For the conquest of happiness sweet;
    Wild seas of ambition whose waves of desire
On their obstacles mighty continually beat,
        Where neither the shore nor the ocean is
            fixed;
    Like thunderous songs of a choir,
Whose murmurs in music repeat;
    And confusion and chaos are terribly mingled
            and mixed.

Dust! Dust! Dust!
Borne in the arms of the gathering gust,
And whirled on the wings of the wind,
The eyes feel the blight of the blind,
And horror comes into the heart;
For nature is far more unkind
Than the thousands that struggle apart.
Dark, wild, inescapable dust,
In fiercest, untamable clouds,
That men into misery helplessly thrust,
And bury in agony-shrouds;
A simoom of sorrow whose pestilent breath
To the strong and the weak, to the young and
the old,
Brings despair that is reckless of possible gain,
And the awfullest anguish of death;
Till the soul in its rage uncontrolled,
Droops low in the horrible sickness and sorrow
of pain.

But out from the clouds,
Out from the agonized dust that enshrouds;
True kings shall arise who shall reign
In homes on the populous plain!
Great cities shall gather and grow
In glories that never shall wane,
Far over the valleys below.
With merry yet measureless might

They conquer the waste with the gladness
that brings
To the desert the newest delight.
The barren shall bloom as the rose, and the land
That is sleeping, a wilderness wasted and
wild,
And dreaming to welcome its master's com-
mand,
Shall leap at the touch of his hand,
His voice shall obey as a child!

"SING ME A SONG, O, WIND."

SING me a song, O, Wind,
Of musical cadence sweet,
Which in the wood around
Shall often and oft repeat;
Soft as an angel's song
That never can give annoy,
Which in the balmy notes
Shall tell me its tales of joy.

Sing me a song, O, Wind,
Of countries beyond the sea,
Which in thy wand'rings oft
Thou pass with a footstep free;

Lands that are ever green
    ' Neath blaze of the tropic spells,
Bright with their blessed suns,
    Where summer forever dwells.

Sing me a song, O, Wind,
    Of groves with a verdure fair,
Waving their boughs of green
    O'er solitudes grand and rare;
Groves with a stillness sweet,
    With cheering and cooling shades,
Where from its cares the race
    May rest in the leafy glades.

Sing me a song, O, Wind,
    Of birds with a plumage gay,
That with their carols sweet
    Give praise to the God of day;
Music of sad refrain,
    Though fond in its tender chime,
Thou in thy travels wide
    Hast heard in a fairy clime.

Sing me a song, O, Wind,
    Of crystalline brooks at play,
Which with the murmurs low
    Make sweetest of sounds all day;

Winding through meadows wide,
  And blossoming fields between,
Fringed with the willows tall
  On emerald banks of green.

Sing me a song, O, Wind,
  Of flowers that are fond and fair,
Filling the fields of earth
  With beauty and fragrance rare;
Wafting an incense pure
  On every breeze that blows,
Drawn from the lily's heart
  And soul of the royal rose.

Sing me a song, O, Wind,
  Of man in his brightest homes;
Tell if he there meet joy,
  Wherever his longing roams;
Tell if there's e'er a place
  Where, all his ambition spent,
He toils throughout all his days
  And knoweth no discontent.

Sing me a song, O, Wind,
  For I am a-weary now;
Life, with its woes and cares,
  Hangs heavily on my brow;

Sing me a song of cheer,
    My heart that is sad to ease;
Sing in thy brightness and joy
    With heavenly harmonies!

A CHRISTMAS CAROL.

THE brazen bells of laughing lands
    In swelling echoes wildly ring,
And over seas and hoary strands
    This Christmas carol sing.

" AWAKEN, O, heart of the race,
    To bountiful riches from Eden above,
Till roses of beauty and lilies of grace
Shall sweeten the languishing bosom with love;
Till virulent sorrow and venomous hate
    Their poisonous curses of misery cease,
And rapturous fortune, felicitous fate,
    Have rule in the musical meadows of peace.

" The voices of morning to men,
    In passionate whispers of bounteous glee,
Are pulsing the gladness of Christmas again
    · O'er plains of the prairie and sounds of the sea;

Rejoice and be happy, O, languishing soul,
　In limitless treasures of marvelous cheer,
Till ravishing murmurs of lullabies roll
　Through all of the sorrows that sadden the year !

" Though summer has gone from the earth,
　And silken embraces of velvety snow
Are folding the blossoms of beauty and worth
　In wretched surroundings of wearisome woe;
Let innocent joys in their sweetness abound
　And silvery cadence in melody start,
Till rapturous fortunes with pleasure surround
　The aims of the soul and the hopes of the heart.

" Let youth with its yearning engage
　All vigorous passion that lives in the breast,
While tearful remembrance of tottering age
　Finds halcyon harbors of comforting rest;
Let silver of years with the ardor of youth
　Be going again through the temple of joy,
While palms of amusment and laurels of truth
　Encircle the hearts of the maiden and boy.

" Let happiness reign with the race;
　There's never a reason for sorrowful tears,
Kriss Kringle has come with his fatherly face
　To comfort complaining humanity's fears;

Let music go 'round and the beautiful smile
  Bring gladsome delight to the bosom of bliss,
Till gentle enjoyments unbroken beguile
  The souls of the sad with their coveted kiss.

" Though crystalline frost on the trees,
  Though ice on the river and snow on the plain
Are freezing the breath of the shivering breeze,
  The heart has Nepenthe for all of its pain;
For Christmas is king, and his bountiful hand
  Is giving its treasures to mountain and lea,
And gentleness rules on the billowy strand,
  And reigns in the far-away isles of the sea."

THIS is the carol that swells
  Over the meadows and brakes,
From brazen throats of the pealing bells
  When Christmas morning wakes.

YEARS THAT ARE TO BE.

WILD years that are to be
    The sad completion of my weary life,
      In ghostly mantles of despairing strife
Your phanton dimness darkly shadows me!
Guant demons dancing from your horrid halls
Entwine my soul in gloomy arms of woe,
While mystic fancies to my madness show
    The monsters on your walls.

Your forms are skeletons,
Whose bony hands with mortal fingers play,
Where grinning skulls are heaping on the way,
And airy specters meet the timid ones;
Death drops his arrows from your sullen skies,
Destruction dances in your noisome shades,
And in the dreadful darkness of your glades
    The horrid shriekings rise.

There in your cycles are
Dark valleys where my weary feet must go,
Though devils of disaster hurl and throw
Their awful sorrows from the fortunes far;
No hands of pleasure can presume to part
The clouded curtains of impending care,
And hissing serpents of insane despair
    Pour poison in my heart.

O, years that are to be,
Among your solitudes I, dreaming, grope;
My life's the shade of unaccomplished hope,
My heart's a ghoul that feeds on agony!
No strains of music call my tears away,
No smiling star illumes the awful night;
Ambition weeps; my soul draws without light
    My shameless feet astray!

No soothing welcome floats
Between your marble lips, nor sweetly rise

The tender songs of gentle melodies
From croaking caverns of your iron throats;
But from your dirges of destructive pain,
Wild clash of wretched sound is borne to me,
Where death and failure, tears and misery,
    In robes of anguish reign.

    But my heart hopes to find
Some infant joy for woes that sorrow did,
Some faded garland on some coffin lid,
To cheer the wildness of my broken mind;
Some angel pleasures in your realms must roll,
Some laughing life, some music, in your glooms,
Shall gladness give, amid your ghostly tombs,
    Mad Future, to my soul!

IF WE DON'T OR IF WE DO.

IF we don't or if we do,
    What's the odds to me and you?
    Fame is e'er a heartless jade,
And her slaves are poorly paid;
Weary hearts and soul's distress
Are the prices of success;
All our stations sadness view,—
If we don't or if we do.

If we don't or if we do,
Our deservings will accrue;
We must pay the fullest price,
For each virtue and each vice,
And each life for every thing
Must an equal portion bring;
Justice shall our deeds review,
If we don't or if we do.

If we don't or if we do,
Fortune to our worth is true;
Trophies that enshroud our clay,
Scarce are worth the price we pay;
Shame doth small endeavors share,
Fame and glory, toil and care;
Earth floats but an equal crew,
If we don't or if we do.

If we don't or if we do,
What's the diff'rence 'tween the two,
When our souls have gone to God
And we sleep beneath the sod?
Kindred grasses wave and creep
Where the prince and pauper sleep;
We shall have our six-feet-two,
If we don't or if we do.

If we don't or if we do,
We but dust and ashes brew;

Labor, trouble, toil and strife
Weave within each human life;
Sorrows cloud the younger years;
Age is bowed with cares and tears;
Accidents in fame are few,—
If we don't or if we do.

If we don't or if we do,
Fate to our deserts is true;
If we fail, or falter not,
Every life deserves his lot;
Every human, small or great,
Buys with current coin his fate;
What's the odds to me and you,
If we don't or if we do?

DEAR SONGS OF MY COUNTRY!

DEAR songs of my country! How sweetly thy
       measures
    Come stealthily stealing o'er mountain and
    wave,
To sweeten the riches of liberty's treasures
  And thrill with their numbers the hearts of the
    brave!

To move in wild glory the souls of a nation,
  Till men are together so happily hurled,
That millions are bound in fraternal relation
  And brotherhoods rule in the ranks of the world.

Such praises ye offer our heroes and sages,
  So grand is the greatness that lives in thy strains,
That small is the fame of the far away ages,
  So sunken in tyranny, fettered in chains.
For freedom ye strive and ye struggle for glory,
  And Liberty—Liberty still is your theme—
And glad are your lips with the national story,
  Which warriors have written on forest and stream.

Dear songs of my country!   The soul patriotic
  Ye fill with the wishes of mighty emprise,
Till conquers he tyranny harsh and despotic,
  Or first in the front of the battle he dies.
Ye offer him laurels, ye crown him with praises,
  Who falls in the fight with his face to the foe,
And gratitude over his sepulcher raises
  The marbles eternal of national woe.

Your strains are as high as the cloud-covered
      mountains,
  As deep as the ocean, as wide as the land,
As pure as the murmurs of silvery fountains,
  But loud as the roar on the billowy strand.

Our deep-furrowed prairies, our ship-laden rivers,
  Our ax-ringing forests, our steam-shrieking bays,
Swell high in your music, for all are free givers
  To freedom's true grandeur and liberty's praise.

How fondly, dear songs of my country, ye cherish
  The struggle heroic, the God-shapen deed,
That nothing of worthiness ever may perish
  But live to the time of humanity's need!
Afar from the realms of the centuries olden,
  Ye summon with gladness the glories of years,
To greet every hero with cadences golden,
  And sing every sage that in greatness appears.

The ages may falter thee, Land of my Birth,
  The years may thy grandeur and glory betray;
But long as thy songs murmur over the earth,
  No forces can carry thy splendors away!
Then live, ye dear songs of my country, forever,
  With voices eternal to utter her name,
That cycles may never her liberty sever,
  Nor trample her greatness nor crumble her fame!

JULY FOURTH.

HAIL, glorious morning of Columbia's birth,
  Celestial dawn of freedom! There shall be
In recognition of thy wondrous worth
By mighty millions this side of the sea,
Triumphant crowns of laurel wreathed for thee!
Welcome thy mammoth pageants, welcome all
  The choral songs and melodies of glee,
The swelling shouts of praise that gladly fall
From mighty multitudes in anthems national!

High hangs the sacred banner, and the stars
  Dance in the sunshine, while the breezes play
Around the glory of the hallowed bars
  Gleaming in white and crimson; music gay
  Floats from the patriot host and cheers array
Great shouts around its foldings. Long in state,
  Flag of the brave and free, wave o'er this day
To bring the world rejoicings which await
The natal hours of might, the day we celebrate!

How fears the tyrant in his capital,
  As myriad wires throb with the nation's tale!
How despot trembles in his castled hall,
  When liberty's wild shouts of power prevail,

And give their gladness unto every gale!
Fetters and chains dissolve in holy trust,
   Scepters and swords in puny weakness fail,
While crowns and thrones make monumental dust,
And kingly Might is dead, Oppression downward
   thrust.

Wide float thy wondrous pæans; loudly range
   Thy songs of holy rapture; and the roars
Of deep-mouthed cannons echo wild and strange
   Through shouting cities; Patriotism pours
   Her full libations on the trembling shores,
Till earth reels with her triumph; and the voice
   Of millions mad with merriment far soars
From sea to ocean with entrancing noise,
Till nations hear the cry and continents rejoice.

Wave on, thou flag of freedom, and this day
   Still live in hearts of nations! O, thou Land,
Where Man was first the monarch, where the sway
   Of birth exalted first was broken, stand
   To guard the helpless with a mighty hand,
And give the weak protection; scout the ban
   Which tyrants utter, and with growing band
Of noble freemen serve thy primal plan,
And bind all nations in the Brotherhood of Man!

"O, GENTLE SHADE OF QUIET WOODS."

O, GENTLE shade of quiet woods,
  Where nature dwells in leafy halls,
  I love the sacred voice that falls
In music o'er thy solitudes!
Within thine arms the weary heart
  Is hidden from the toils of men,
And pleasure makes ambition start
  Into a nobler life again.

Among the fragrant shadows throng
  With all the riches of their truth,
  Glad echoes from the days of youth
And mingle into laughing song;
While angel fingers touch the keys
  That slumber in the silent breast,
Till mem'ry wakes her lullabies
  And childhood fancies rock to rest.

Again the hours of early joy
  Upon the aged years intrude,
  And dance amid the summer wood
The golden dreamings of the boy;

Again the songs of wonder thrill
   The days of life with gladness wild,
And lofty visions fondly fill
   The longing fancies of the child.

Enchanted choirs of baby years,
   Sweet dirges from the cradle's keys,
   The glories of your harmonies
Impel my secret soul to tears!
The roses of my fancies fade
   Into the dust of wicked strife,
And all the promise boyhood made
   Has proved the desert of my life.

O, fragrant woods of happy times,
   Fair children of the glowing days,
   How sweet the music of your lays
Is mingled into fairy chimes!
Ye lisp again the songs of yore,
   The stories of my infant years,
And throw a sweeter cadence o'er
   My hoary sorrows and my tears!

LOVE.

ANGELIC theme of ancient lays!
   By Doric hills, Athenian vales,
  The nations bound thy brows with bays
  And fanned thy cheeks with scented gales;
While golden lamps illumed thy shrines
  Beside the Tiber and the Po,
  Till anthems thine were taught to flow
Along the Alps and Appenines.

The souls of sages and of slaves
  Were faithful servants unto thee,
Whose rapture soothed the Grecian waves,
  And kissed the islands of the sea;
And bounding on from strand to strand
  It crossed the coasts and climbed the slopes,
  To place a crown of tender hopes
Upon the vine-clad Roman land.

Great empress of that early time,
  Glad ruler of the gentle souls,
Each year is changed to raptured rhyme
  That o'er thy laughing bosom rolls;

For cycles as they sink to rest
    So closely guard thy joy and truth,
    That fondness and immortal youth
Give sweet embraces to thy breast.

Thou goddess of the.Paphian shrine,
    Cytheran queen of Ion's isle,
Fair Venus from the land of wine,
    The races love thy dewy smile;
While silent hills and dewy glades
    Bear praises on each breeze that blows,
    Sweet as the breath of morning rose
That blossoms in the woodland shades!

Then crown, O, Love, these later days
    With mystic charms of wondrous bliss,
That lived when thou wert wreathed with bays,
    And nations hungered for thy kiss!
No more thy temples tower above,
    But lives and bosoms hold thee dear;
    Then come with all thy worth of cheer
And gentleness, O, mighty Love!

WINTERS ON THE FARM.

GLAD winters on the olden farm!
    How raptures from those early times
    Commingle into fairy chimes
Which gently banish cries of harm!
    My fainting soul finds rest the whiles
Within the arms of memory,
And tender scenes of boyish glee
    Transform my sorrows into smiles.

How brightly beamed the pleasures then,
    When frigid fingers came to throw
    A wintry winding sheet of snow
Around the silent homes of men!
But happiness found no alarm,
    For safe with cheer, secure with love,
    She gladly grew and sweetly throve
Through winters on the olden farm.

With merry bells and busy sleighs,
    That sung and flew o'er icy vales
    And climbed the hills as fleet as gales,
Like singing phantoms died the days;

Or then with coat and muffler warm
  Sweet children glided on the lake,
  Or chased.the rabbit through the brake,
In winters on the olden farm.

How glad the joys at eventide
  When 'round the hearth-stone's pleasant heat
  The simple song in music sweet
From loving voices floated wide!
The mellowed apples gave a charm,
  While pop-corn white and cider bright
  With worlds of laughter lent delight
To winters on the olden farm.

Thrice happy nights and happy days,
  Sweet isles of pleasure in the past,
  May long your hallowed moments cast
A sacred sunshine o'er my ways!
And where life leads me, gladly arm
  My soul with angel songs of bliss,
  With true embrace and holy kiss,
O, winters on the olden farm!

"O, WEAK AND WEARY WORLD!"

O WEAK and weary world
 Forever struggling on,
 When will thy toils in comfort be
 impearled,
 When will thy sorrows and thy cares be gone?
When shall the races, all ambition dead,
 Forsake the stony slope and rocky steep,
And in contentment sweetly wed
 The joys that never sleep?

O, weak and weary world,
 Long hast thou toiled in vain;
The smoky fumes of woe are darkly curled
 With endless troubles and enduring pain;
When will thy bosom, faint and helpless grown,
 Rest sweetly in the balmy bowers of ease?
Avoid the woes that constant groan
 And follow shapes that please?

O, weak and weary world,
 Why search the hills and seas?
All Nature is in secrecy enfurled
 And thou canst never solve her mysteries;

Thou canst not understand nor comprehend
  Her varied movements nor the intricate,
The systems that so far extend,
  Creation wide and great.

  O, weak and weary world,
    Why more attempt advance ?
Long have thy forces in confusion whirled
  In circles through the misty maze of chance;
The nations rise and sink in sepulchres,
  Thy peoples perish in a common grave;
Progression dies, perfection errs,
  Wrong rules the wood and wave.

  O, weak and weary world,
    Let thy ambition rest!
Long have defeat and gloomy ruin twirled
  In dark embrace the purest and the best;
Destruction is thy portion, death thy part,
  Ashes thy glory, and thy splendor dust;
Then ease the longings of thy breast;
  Serve pleasures well; and trust!

EX ANIMA.

THE gloomy hours of silence wake
    Remembrance and her train,
      And phantoms through the fancies chase
  The mem'ries that remain;
And hidden in the dark embrace
  Of days that now are gone,
I see a form, a fairy form,
  And fancy hurries on!

I see the old familiar smile,
  I hear the tender tone,
I greet the softness of the glance
  That cheered me when alone;
The ruby chains of rich romance
  That bound our bosoms o'er,
I still can know, I still can feel,
  As they were felt before.

I name the vows, the fresh young vows,
  That we together said;
What matters it ? She can not know;
  She slumbers with the dead!

Again the fields of fate I sow,
  As she and I have sown;
I dream again the same old dreams,
  But I am left alone!

The twining grasses verdant wreathe
  Above her silent grave;
The rose and violet over all
  Their purest blossoms wave;
Unbidden from their fountains fall
  The tender tides of tears;
A sorrow winds among the days,
  And chains the passing years.

My life commingles shine with shade,
  The lily with the rose,
And in my heart a loathsome weed
  Beside each lily grows;
Through every thought, through every deed,
  The somber shadows play;
And I am sad, alone and sad,
  And life is never gay.

"LO, ALL THE AGE IS RANK WITH WRONG."

L O, all the age is rank with wrong!
   The nations kneel to monstrous might,
   And horrid cries that haunt the night,
Have hushed the notes of happy song;
Mankind the deepest truth has missed,
   The best emotions have grown dim;
We praise the God that dwelt in Christ,
   But crucify the man in him.

Laws, noble, good, and great at first,
   With plan perverted, bind again
   The regal rights of mind and men
And prove of tyrants far the worst;
With blinded eyes is Nature made,
   And knows her constant purpose crossed,
While crafty Jacob plies his trade
   And Esau finds his blessing lost.

Earth yields her fruits in ample store;
   Her children all are heirs that trace
   Their lineage through the royal race,
And all her wealth is theirs—and more;

But one with cunning hand controls
    The portions that his brothers fed,
While thousands—just and worthy souls—
    In aimless anguish cry for bread!

No royal blood by caste or creed,
    No pride of place, no gild of gold
    Can warm the weak, accursed with cold,
Or light the awful nights of need;
Labor alone can blessings bring
    To crown the brows of freedom's brave;
The toiler is the truest king,
    The idler is the only slave!

But laugh, O, Labor, dry thy tears!
    A better day is drawing nigh;
    Hope brightens all the somber sky;
The golden age of Love is near!
Behold!   But yonder stands a Star!
    The ancient lies are downward hurled;
A man—a child—is greater far
    Than all the wealth of all the world!

"LOVE, THOU GAYEST FANCY-WEAVER."

LOVE, thou gayest fancy-weaver,
　　Heart-betrayer, soul-deceiver,
　　Come with all thy clinging kisses;
Bringing all thy beaming blisses;
It may serve the cynic's parts,
　　If he curse and if he scout thee,
But, O, where were gentle hearts,
　　If they had to live without thee!

Weave the spells of thy beguiling
'Round and 'round me with thy smiling,
Till the ashen cheek is beaming,
And the faded eye is gleaming;
Millions may endure the fight
　　In the battle vain to end thee,
But when taste they thy delight
　　They will serve thee and defend thee.

Bring thy little winsome graces
And the sweets of glad embraces,
Till the pleasures all are dancing
Into mazy whirls entrancing;

It may please the icy breast
  To despise thee and distress thee,
But the burning hearts find rest
  When they bless thee and caress thee.

Send thy gladness, laughing rover,
All my sorrows o'er and over,
Till the strains of happy pleasure
Mingle in melodious measure;
It may give a transient glee
  To condemn thy ways and sever,
But the sweets of melody
  Thou wilt murmur on forever.

Bind my heart in silken chaining,
Till from thee is none remaining;
Clothe my soul in glad completeness
Of thy happiness and sweetness;
When the times are true, the soul
  May not hunger for thy gladness,
But when surging sorrows roll
  Thou alone shalt banish sadness.

THE FARMER.

L ET nations encircle the brows of the brave
 With glory the greatest that glitters below,
 Who make in the blood of the battle a grave
For all that are found in the ranks of the foe;
But I from the greatness, the grandeur, and gleam,
 Would turn to the light of clear-glowing hearth,
And choose from his joy for the soul of my theme
The farmer, the lord and the king of the earth.

Let millions give worship to riches and wealth,
 That gay in their brilliancy sparkle and gleam,
And serve with the hands of their happiest health
 The haughty who idle and revel and dream;
In hall or in hamlet, in cottage or cave,
 Or sickened with sorrow or maddened with mirth,
There's none I shall serve with the will of a slave
 But the farmer, the lord and the king of the earth.

Let poets in praises heart-swelling and sweet
 With rapture that rises in beautiful song,
Make sages immortal and ages replete
 With hundreds of heroes who wrestled the wrong;

All honest men well from the Muses may claim
  The numbers that murmur to merit and worth,
And so I would fold in the mantles of fame
  The farmer, the lord and the king of the earth.

Let orators over the deeds of the great
  Re-echo the tributes of tenderest praise,
And over the ashes that slumber in state
  Let peoples their marbles and monuments raise;
But I, from the frenzied applauses uncouth,
  To those who are chained in the bondage of birth,
Would flee to surround with the lilies of truth
  The farmer, the lord and the king of the earth.

Let hearts that are grateful in gratitude crown
  The friend of the many and foe of the few;
Let souls in their secret admiring enthrone
  Whatever a martyr or minion may do;
But down in my bosom while reasonings reign,
  Of friendship and love there is never a dearth
For him who is toiling in pleasure or pain,
  The farmer, the lord and the king of the earth.

"NATURE HAS A THOUSAND CHOIRS."

NATURE has a thousand choirs
    Singing in the sylvan shadows,
And the music of her lyres
·   Echoes in the merry meadows;
Always glad with golden glee
Sounds her happy melody,
Swelling wild in fairy measure
With the songs of purest pleasure.

Where the dancing fountains play
    Winding warbles shake and shiver,
And soft carols rise alway
    From the ripples of the river;
Sweetest voices fondly call
From the fleecy waterfall,
And the joyful chimes are creeping
Where the lovely lake is sleeping.

Raptures echo in the wood,
    Where the pimpernel reposes;
Gladness fills the solitude
    Where the blushes kiss the roses;

Sunny beam and somber gloom
Utter hymns from bowers of bloom,
Where the vernal winds are crying
And the vocal birds are flying.

O'er the smiling scenes of earth
    Nature throws no sullen weather;
All her soul is full of mirth,
    Song and springtime walk together;
For the harps of happy days
Wake the woodlands with their lays,
And where lilies white are springing
Gentle melodies are ringing.

O, wild Nature, from thy soul
    Fill the human hearts with gladness,
Till their lives shall gladly troll
    Songs that banish all their sadness !
Bathe their breasts with songs of love
From the Edens found above,
Till their lips shall sing the story
Of their happiness and glory !

THE WORKINGMAN.

GOD bless the brawny arms of toil,
  The noble hearts and royal hands,
    That plow the plain and seed the soil,
    And grow the grains of laughing lands !
King in the blessed vales of life
  Where perfect pleasures first began,
May blessings come with raptures rife
  To crown the humble workingman !

His kingdoms wave with bannered corn
  And meadows bright with fairy bloom,
While duties of his heart are born
  Where sylvan shadows hide the gloom;
Sweet Nature fills his heart with health,
  While rustic warbles lead his soul
Where rill and fountain sing by stealth
  And breezes soft with music roll.

He lives where simple wishes throng,
  And give contentment to his breast,
While tender lullabies of song
  Bring angel gladness to his rest;

No praises linger o'er his name
  Where he in silence works apart,
And honor never links with fame
  The modest glories of his heart.

He needs no kiss of royal crown
  To wield the axe or guide the plow,
Or woo the smiles of heaven down
  To cling in clusters on his brow;
But in the sacred shine of love,
  With humble deeds he lives his days,
And, drinking from the founts above,
  He scatters gladness o'er his ways.

Proud monarch of the tattered vest,
  Thy toil is fraught with greater gains
Than his that bleeds where warrior crest
  Slays thousands on the battled plains !
Thy duty prompts to build, to grow,
  The forest fell, the city plan
And scatter seeds of love below,
  Where'er thou art, O, workingman!

GIVING AND FORGIVING.

'TIS not by selfish miser's greed
 The great rewards of love are given;
'Tis not the cynic's haughty creed
Which gladly makes this world a heaven;
But tender word and loving deed
 Increase the angel joys of living,
And mortals gain life's grandest meed
 By acts of giving and forgiving.

Let warriors bold with armies fight
 Their awful battles brave and gory,
To reap the harvest of their might
 And fill a gaping world with glory!
The humble heroes, out of sight,
 Where hidden tears and woes are striving,
Win victories for truth and right
 By deeds of giving and forgiving.

Let mighty kings of loyal lands
 Despise the faithful sons of duty,
And with the swords of vandal hands
 Destroy the homes of joy and beauty;

The honest lords of low commands
  Will find a nobler way of thriving,
In lonely vales where sorrow stands,
  By sweets of giving and forgiving.

Let rich men with their heaps of gold
  Be servants of the shining splendor,
And crush the bosom, poor and old,
  That lives by mercies pure and tender;
But still the soul with saints enrolled
  Will keep its charity surviving,
And have its humble glory told
  In tales of giving and forgiving.

O, helping hands and Christian hearts,
  Twin parents of the race's gladness,
God speed the time when your sweet arts
  Shall banish every sign of sadness !
When mournful cries, when pain's wild darts,
  Shall cease to curse the days of living,
And Heaven's love to man imparts
  The joys of giving and forgiving.

"O, SACRED SOULS THAT GRANDLY SING."

O SACRED souls that grandly sing
The secret songs of human hearts,
Where your wild music madly starts,
The sorrows into raptures spring !
Within the warbles of your chimes
Man reads the longings of his days,
And finds, amid your lofty lays,
Glad music for his gloomy times.

How sweet the mute, melodious cries
Which only lives like yours may hear,
Where pleasures thrill the singer's ear
With laughing strains of lullabies !
You know soft voices, rich with love,
That mingle in the fields and woods,
To bless the silent solitudes
With carols coming from above.

Your golden harps resound alway,
Where valley bound with blossom lies,
And rugged mountains highest rise,
And silver fountains softly play ;

While in the gladness of your songs
  The fainting bosoms hope again,
  And toil among their fellow men,
Forgetful of their ancient wrongs.

You sport with singing meadows bright,
  With fragrant winds and scented gales,
  Where shine and shadow kiss the vales
In fairy fondness of delight ;
For where the meads and forests blend,
  The sweetest songs of life are found,
  And where the lonely hills abound
The soul of music meets a friend.

Glad hearts that warble songs divine,
  Sweet singers of a mourning race,
  The ages long your brows shall grace
With crowns where bays and laurels twine !
For man the grandest garland brings,
  To bless the tender lives that tell,
  And with their mystic music swell,
The lays that Nature fondly sings !

CHRISTMAS TIME.

HOW sweet the brazen belfries chime
 Across the hills and through the dales,
 And o'er the breasts of meadowed vales,
Beneath the smiles of Christmas time !
Rough sorrow's thorny fingers grow
 As soft and waxen as a child's,
 And balmy pleasures o'er the wilds
Chant music to the drifting snow.

Ah, scattered locks that fringe my face,
 With wintry wisps of white and gray !
 Ah, sad, dimmed eyes that look away
To artless childhood's tender grace !
To-night those years with joys sublime
 Steal over me and fill my soul
 With lullabies of bliss that roll
The golden glees of Christmas time.

Again I live in wondrous days,
 When baby hands with chubby glee
 Plucked gladness from the loaded tree
Where loving burdens bent the sprays ;

The sunny songs of that sweet clime
  Sing softly in my soul again,
  Till I forget the ways of men
And laugh and shout at Christmas time.

Angelic joys that died in pain,
  Sweet raptures from the days of bliss,
  Your loving lips with clinging kiss
Thrill all my heart and soul and brain ;
And turning from my weary rhyme
  To count my sorrows o'er and o'er,
  I'd give my life to know once more
Those wondrous days of Christmas time.

Ring, laughing bells, ring out to-night !
  From happy years that now are fled,
  You bring the faces of the dead,
And bless me with a deep delight !
Away, away, these thoughts of men,
  These toils of mine, that sadness give ;
  My heart grows young and I would live
My Christmas pleasures o'er again !

TRUEST HEROES ARE UNKNOWN.

ALL worthies are not sung in song,
    That live their lives and do their deeds
    Where wounded nature writhes and bleeds
Beneath the savage blows of wrong ;
From humble duties tender grown,
The truest heroes are unknown.

The heart that toils where none may know
    And uncomplaining conquers care,
    To save his loved ones or to spare
His fellows from the pangs of woe,
Is more the hero than who shields
His country on the bleeding fields.

He claims no praises for his love,
    He seeks no tribute for his worth,
    But sows the desert hearts of earth
With blossoms from the vales above ;
And in their sunshine warm and bright
He holds these duties as his right.

Where lives are dark with dismal groans
    Great men are often chained by fate,
    And oft are slaves more truly great
Than princes on their purple thrones ;

But servant brows are bound with shame,
While monarchs flutter into fame.

Deeds pure and noble, gladly done,
   Unselfish work for sickly souls
   When sorrow in black surges rolls
And gloomy darkness hides the sun,—
These in their truth make more the man
Than royal aim or princely plan.

But sometime man shall rule by thought,
   And worth shall gain her just return,
   Till all shall every singer spurn   .
Who in the ancient cycles taught
That heroes rest in royal graves,
But never in the tombs of slaves.

IF WE BUT KNEW.

IF we but knew the weary way,
   The poisoned paths of hostile hate,
   The roughened roads of fiercest fate,
Through which our brother's journey lay,
Would we condemn, as now we do,
His faults and failures,—if we knew?

Would we forget the shadows grim,
  The lonely hours of grief and pain,
  The follies dead, the pleasures slain,
The tears and toils that hindered him,
And only prize the deeds that grew
To mighty conquest, if we knew?

Would careless hand sow tares of strife,
  Amid the blooms of happy care,
  And plant, in spite of sigh and prayer,
Wild thorns amid the blameless life,
Till sorrows rule the nations through,
With scarce a rival, if we knew?

Would we be quicker with our praise,
  And gladly give the greatest meeds
  As recompense for noble deeds,
And heroes crown with brightest bays,
And slay all foes that hearts imbue
With doubt and weakness, if we knew?

From lofty kings would constant worth
  On peasant brows their crowns bestow,
  And rising from her overthrow
Eternal justice rule the earth,
While right would strip the favored few
To bless the many, if we knew?

If we but knew !   Ah, well-a-day !
   From lives that murmur, full of ills,
   Behind the shadows of the hills,
God hides our brother's heart away;
And we shall know in vales of rest
That His eternal ways are best !

HOPE.

WHEN man from pure perfection fell,
   And bathed his life in grief and woe,
   His angel heart had overthrow
From all the joys he loved so well,
And only Hope of all the host
Remained to comfort him when lost.

And when the other passions throw
   Their phantoms in the arms of death,
   And pour their last remaining breath
Within the dismal haunts of woe,
Then Hope alone of all remains
To soothe our sorrows and our pains.

Hope makes the fearful millions brave,
   The helpless and the weary strong,
   Gives courage to the fainting throng
And whispers freedom to the slave,

And unto each, where'er he lives,
Unceasing cause to struggle gives.

In heavy hours of ghostly gloom
  When raging billows dash and beat
  Around the weak and weary feet
Which tremble on the yawning tomb,
The harp of Hope divinely sings
Exalted songs of better things.

It lifts the gaze of mortal eyes
  Above the desert and the dearth,
  Above the barren fields of earth,
Unto the promise of the skies,
And to the last expiring breath
Gives comfort in the hour of death.

O, sacred light of human life,
  Eternal star of Heaven's love,
  Thy brightness ever shines above
The darkest hours of woe and strife,
To raise our souls above the sod
Into the holy home of God !

DESPONDENCY.

O, GLOOMY world that rolls in weary space,
    And moans wild music to the broken spheres,
      Whose rivers wander into seas of tears,
Despair has bound thee in a close embrace;
    A birth, a life, a death; man is no more!

Death grows beside existence, and with time
    Is comrade of its changes; cycles roll
      Their heavy circles through the human soul,
And pour their dirges into mournful rhyme;
    A birth, a life, a death; man is no more!

He gropes in shadows for a happy beam
    That shall delight his bosom; into mist
      Dissolves the substance that ambition kissed,
While greatness grows the garland of a dream;
    A birth, a life, a death; man is no more!

Endeavor struggles to an open grave;
    The past is lost in monumental dust,
      Where age on age in angry ire has thrust
The wise, the strong, the mighty, and the brave;
    A birth, a life, a death; man is no more!

The years are shades that totter from their tombs,
  The ages, ghosts that live in catacombs
  And lure the Present to their awful homes,
Where ancient races wander in the glooms;
    A birth, a life, a death; man is no more !

Oblivion welcomes men with gentle arms,
  And presses them like infants to her breast,
  Repeats to them her lullabies of rest,
And guards them from all sorrows and alarms;
    A birth, a life, a death; man is no more !

Then hasten, world, and let my battle cease;
  I care not where I stay nor when I go;
  For action gives unhappiness and woe,
But Lethe brings forgetfulness and peace;
    A birth, a life, a death; man is no more !

IF LOVE WERE KING.

IF Love were king,
  That sacred Love which knows not selfish
    pleasure,
But for its children spends its fondest treasure,
      Sad hearts would sing,
And all the hosts of misery and wrong
Forget their anguish in the happy song
      That joy would bring.

      If Love were king,
Gaunt wickedness would hide his loathsome feat-
    ures,
And virtue would to all the world's sad creatures
      Her treasures fling;
Till drooping souls would rise above their fate,
And find sweet flowers for all the desolate
      And sorrowing.

      If Love were king,
Before the scepter of his might should vanish
Toil's curse and care, and happiness should banish
      Want's awful sting;
While laughing plenty from sweet hands would throw
Delightful raptures over all below,
      And gladness bring.

If Love were king,
The nations would eternal sunshine borrow,
And conquer all the heavy clouds of sorrow
And every thing
That binds the race in groans and agony;
Life's changing seasons would forever be
Unvaried spring.

If Love were king!
O, broken feet that wander worn and weary
Beneath the crags and awful mountains dreary,
With rapture cling
Your anguished arms about him; drink delight
Upon his perfect bosom soft and white
And comforting!

"SING ME THE OLD SONGS, MOTHER."

OUR souls are the deserts of sorrow,
    Our hearts are the ashes of hope,
    And madly from gladness we borrow
    The brightness where sadness may grope;
My raptures in wretchedness vanish,
    My bosom is weeping with wrongs;
Then sing me the old songs, mother,
    Then sing me the dear old songs.

My joys are in memory lying,
  Still ardently happy with youth,
When smiles in ambition were dying,
  And life was the vision of youth;
My brow for your gentle caresses
  And kisses of tenderness longs;
Then sing me the old songs, mother,
  Then sing me the dear old songs.

Sweet murmurs in mystical measures
  Come soothingly over my soul,
Where voices of babyish pleasures
  And echoes of lullabies roll;
The struggles of all my endeavor
  Are bound in the darkest of thongs;
Then sing me the old songs, mother,
  Then sing me the dear old songs.

I fain would return in my dreaming
  To years that proclaimed me a boy,
When gladness was happily beaming
  And life was a musical toy;
My sorrow has never Nepenthe,
  My woe in its bitterness throngs;
Then sing me the old songs, mother,
  Then sing me the dear old songs.

TWO LIVES.

TWO infants in their cradles lie,
   Where lullabies of peace
   In gentle strains of tender music die,
And carols never cease.

Two urchins o'er the meadow lands
   Are bounding in their plays,
Where sweet enjoyment with angelic hands
   Winds gladness o'er the days.

Two boys, where golden fancies bless,
   Repose in sunny beams,
And muse away the hours of happiness
   On couches made of dreams.

Two men upon a summer sea
   Are toiling, brave and strong,
Where pleasures roll their elfin harmony
   And labor ends in song.

Two gray-haired sages, silvered o'er,
   In life meet once again,
To name the wondrous happiness they bore
   Among their fellow-men.

Two graves forever hide the twain
  Who found, in all their years,
No secret shadows, where unbroken pain
  Held fountains full of tears.

Two lives have passed from human reach,
  And few have heard of them,
But joy had not been better served if each
  Had worn a diadem.

Ah, bosoms here are strangely blest
  With perfect bliss that glows,
And he above all others lives the best,
  Who has the fewest woes!

"AWAY, AWAY, FROM THE SULTRY WAYS."

AWAY, away, from the sultry ways
  Where the pleasures fall and fade,
  To the bannered corn and the meadowed
    bloom
And the forest's cooling shade !

Afar, afar, from the rooms of care
  With the toils of life distressed,
To the grassy hills and the fragrant slopes
  And the quiet vales of rest !

Away from the weary, dusty town,
   Where the sorrows dim the days,
To the sleeping lake and the silent stream
   And the wildwood's tangled ways !

To margins wide of the woodland pools,
   Where the wild birds troll their songs,
Where the lilies laugh and the willows wave,
   And the pleasures dance in throngs !

The dark-eyed nymphs and the fairy elves
   In their robes of laughing smiles,
In the forests romp 'neath the leafy trees,
   Through the narrow long-drawn aisles.

The bannered corn and the golden wheat
   In the ties of bliss are bound;
The sweetest joys and highest hopes
   On the shady farms are found.

The raptures reign in the holy scenes,
   And the old grow young once more,
To roam the meadows and live again
   In the happy years of yore.

Then haste, O, haste, to the country downs,
   Where the valleys are sweet with joys,
And the soul grows young, and the heart is light,
   And the bosom is like a boy's !

SPINSTERHOOD.

ALONE, alone, in the twilight gray,
    In the shadows so dark and dim,
  I watch through all of the weary hours,
    And I wait with my heart for him;
For him who'll come, when he comes at all,
    As my king and warrior bold;
Whose form so tall is my fortress wall
    And whose heart is a chunk of gold.

Again, again, do I dream the dreams,
    All the dreams that my young heart knew,
And through my soul do the yearnings thrill
    As of old they were wont to do;
I know in truth when his face I see,
    I shall fall at his shining feet,
Where'er it be and whoever is he,
    In the light of his glances sweet.

I wait in vain for the sounds that rise
    From the tread of his horse's hoof,
And still the mists hide his form away
    And forever he stays aloof;

His shining face and his eyes so bright
    In the shades of the distance hide,
And out of the night with the stars bedight
    He hath never approached my side !

O, years, O, wonderful tide of years,
    From the shadows of time set free
My king, my lover, my life, and bring
    To my heart what is most of me !
Somewhere in pain do his yearnings grope
    For the joys that my love would bring;
O, up the slope of his life-long hope,
    Guide the feet of my royal king!

"SWEET FAIRIES FROM THE ISLES OF SONG."

SWEET fairies from the isles of song,
    Bewitching choirs from music land,
    The pleasures of your wondrous band
Once wooed me from the ways of wrong;
Once won my heart with fond caress
    To sacred vales of summer glees,
    Till carols fraught with lullabies
Filled all my soul with blessedness !

My yearnings miss those gentle sprites,
　Whose laughing lips and angel eyes
　And voices ever winsome-wise,
Bedewed my dreams with new delights;
For in the sad hours of my pain
　I hold them as I hold the dead,
　And trust that in the vales they tread,
My hands shall clasp their hands again.

From those glad meadows where they play
　'Neath lovely sun and gentle star,
　My longing soul has wandered far
On rocky path and thorny way;
I croon again the notes of song
　In strains they taught me years ago,
　And weep because my sorrows know
They have been absent for so long.

Return, O, laughing sprites of rest,
　From gentle isles and peaceful seas,
　And pour the balsamed wine of ease
Upon the anguish of my breast !
Till gladness in her raptures roll
　Sweet strains of music, and I gain
　Eternal joy for all the pain
That darkens o'er my weary soul !

STANZAS.

GOD bless the man who gave us rest
   And him who taught us play,
  For kindness reigned within his breast
  To all our sorrow slay;
The weary heart, the fainting limb,
   The soul that droops in woe,
Should most unceasing praise on him
   In gratitude bestow.

He is the hero of the race,
   The toiling nation's friend,
For pity smiles upon his face
   With joys that never end;
He tears away the iron gyves
   That chain our best repose,
And makes the deserts of our lives
   To blossom as the rose.

He pours his balms into the wound
   Of bosom weak and sad,
Till holy pleasures flit around
   And all the heart is glad;

Till all is sweet·that here before
    Was wrapped in bitter woe,
And only gladness hurries o'er
    The millions here below.

Great man he is, and him I give
    That gratitude of mine,
Which must in brilliance while I live
    With brightest glory shine,
To wreathe a radiance always gay
    Around the worthy breast
Of him who first discovered play
    And gave the nations rest.

MAKE THE MOST OF THIS LIFE.

MAKE the most of this life; where the shadow
        reposes
    The beams of the summer shall gather in glee,
And the snow on the graves of the lilies and roses
    But cradles the blooms that shall whiten the lea;
Though the hopes of the heart be encircled with
        sorrow
And billows of wretchedness mutter and roll,
There shall come with the morn of the bountiful
        morrow
    The pleasures that gladden the desolate soul.

Make the most of this life; where the carols are
    sleeping
That rose in their rapture from lips of the spring,
That awakened the world from its winter of weeping,
    Sweet songs shall be sung by the birds on the
    wing.
Though the bosom be dark with the dirges of sad-
    ness
And solitudes gather so heavy and lone,
There shall float from the musical meadows of
    gladness
The ravishing measures that banish each groan.

Make the most of this life; 'tis a garden of beauty,
    Where, blushing, the blossoms grow tenderly
    sweet,
While they brighten the years of man's labor and
    duty
And scatter the kisses of love at his feet;
'Tis a world that is wild with the laughter of living
    When hands do the brotherly kindness they can,
And its hearts are the treasures of tenderness giving
    To soften and sweeten the nature of man.

Make the most of this life; there is happiness in it,
    When souls find a theme for their jubilant song;
There is music, when angels are taught to begin it,
    Which never was marred with a murmur of wrong;

There are voices thät sing in their sweetness forever,
  And mutter no strains of contention or strife,
Neither burden the hours with the pangs of endeavor,
  When we, with our deeds, make the most of this
    life.

"THE SONGS THAT MOTHER USED TO SING."

THE songs that mother used to sing!
    How tenderly those ditties rcll,
    And to the dirges in my soul
The happy notes of gladness bring!
Where'er my vagrant feet may roam
From pleasures of my childhood's home,
This life of mine with rapture throngs,
When thinking of my mother's songs.

They were not made of magic lays;
    No perfect melodies were found,
    That with the strains of fairy sound
Would charm the stranger's ear to praise;
But I can never hope to meet
Another music half so sweet,
And all my longing love will cling
To songs that mother used to sing.

With gentleness of crooning cries,
   She freed the aching limbs from pain,
   And lulled the eyes to sleep again
With sweetness of her lullabies.
Love mingled with her tender voice
In tones that made the heart rejoice,
And Heaven's music seemed to ring
In songs that mother used to sing.

Though years have passed, they still impart
   Glad warbles to the hours of woe,
   And their mute carols fondly throw
The sacred raptures o'er my heart;
Until my locks are thin and gray
Deep in my soul will sound alway,
And full of joy will ever spring
The songs that mother used to sing.

"QUAFF THE GLASS, THE WINE IS RED."

QUAFF the glass, the wine is red,
   And the rose of youth is glowing,
   While the toils of life are fled
And the snows of age are going;
Quaff it with a hearty will,
   Quaff it deep and quaff forever;
Wine will every sorrow kill,
   And destroy the pleasures never.

When the heart beats sad and low,
  Drink its gladness like a river;
When the soul is weak with woe,
  Quaff and be a cheerful liver;
Never, never, life, despair,
  While a cup of hope is nigh thee;
Bend not under loads of care
  While the fount of joy is by thee!

If the fickle friendships end
  And thy fortune be a sad one,
Claim, O, claim, as truest friend,
  Ruby wine, the sweet and glad one!
If thy love hath proven cold,
  Leave her, leave her, for the new one;
Wine is never false for gold;
  Friend to friend, a tried and true one!

Let the cynics curse and rave;
  This must be a life of pleasure;
Fill a bumper!   He's the knave
  Who would scorn joy's fullest measure;
Quaff the glass, the wine is red;
  Hour by hour the days are going;
Wine is yet the fountain head
  From which pleasure's tide is flowing

GOOD-NIGHT.

GOOD NIGHT, my little love, good-night!
   May angels keep
  With fondest watch thy slumbers, till the light
    Shall break thy sleep,
And morning with its wonders bright
Shall banish all thy cares with might.

Within this quickened life of mine,
   I bear away
The loving looks and tender words of thine,
   Which from this day
Within my soul shall ever shine
And make me better, more divine.

With love and trust and truth, my heart
   Beats all for thee;
And though our lives may wander far apart,
   'Till death's decree
Shall pierce my hopes with deadly dart,
Thou still my star of guidance art.

Good-night, dear one!   As gladdest songs,
   The sweetest dreams
Fill all my happy soul in joyous throngs,
   And tender themes

Bring bliss for which my nature longs,
And slay the curse of ancient wrongs.

Good-night, my little love !   In care
        Of Heaven rest,
And may thy life no deeper sorrow share
        Than love's behest,
Beneath the smiles of raptures rare !
Good-night !   God keep thee everywhere !

LIVE LIFE WITH LOVE.

THERE is no soul of anguish or repining,
    That doubts and trembles in the shades of
        gloom,
But love can lead where softest suns are shining
    And fill his days with beauty and its bloom.
        Live life with love!

There is no bosom dark with lonely caring,
    That sadly sorrows in the nights of woe,
But love can soothe his torture and despairing,
    And scatter gladness where his feet may go.
        Live life with love!

There is no scene of misery or sorrow
That droops and withers in the dark of night,
But love can bring fond yearnings for the morrow
And heap the heart with hope's unfading light.
Live life with love!

There is in all the world no sinful creature
That gropes and falters on his troubled way,
But love can overcome his erring nature,
And change his darkness to eternal day.
Live life with love!

Sweet love, with bounties that her hands are giving,
Can blossom roses on the desert heath,
Can brighten all the longings of the living
And with found kisses warm the lips of death.
Live life with love!

As love is thine, so shall thy days be sweeter
With all the deeds that shall thy fellows bless;
Thy small achievements nobler and completer
With truth and hope and highest happiness!
Live life with love!

DISCONTENT.

THE sun comes up in the east
　　And the sun goes down in the west,
　　And man to me is a heartless beast
And the world has only a savage breast.

How thoughts rush over my soul
　　As the waves walk over the sea !
Their forms flee soon and the sorrows roll
　　In the deep distress that is over me.

How hopes arise in my heart,
　　As the roses bloom over the plain!
But time is tearing their sweets apart
　　And they die in darkness and awful pain.

Ambitions burn in my breast,
　　As the fires in a city rage;
But damp creeps over their fervid zest
　　And they sink away into ashen age.

If there was pleasure for pain
　　I could well be happy awhile,
And, O, my bosom would ne'er complain,
　　If my fortune gave me a single smile.

But here I am, and the curse is on,
And my life is a waste of woe,
And ere one river of tears is gone,
O, another torrent begins to flow.

Ah, the sun comes up in the east
And the sun goes down in the west,
And man to me is a heartless beast
And the world has only a savage breast!

STANZAS.

O, PUT not trust nor tenderness to sleep,
In sorrow sad;
The heart, in which a little love may creep,
Is not all bad.

The darkest hours that wear a wondrous gloom,
Are somewhat light,
If but one ray of brilliancy illume
The brooding night.

The field in which the weed and bramble thrive
Has some of good,
If but a single blossom struggling live
Amid the rude.

The ocean vast is not all desolate,
          The worlds between,
If on its waters bearing human freight
          One sail is seen.

All is not harsh and cold amid the wood,
          If warbled song
Resound, how feebly, through the solitude
          Of tangled wrong.

The desert, barren, bleak, a waste of sand
          Does never spread,
If spear of grass in verdure green expand
          Above the dead.

Then put not trust nor tenderness to sleep
          In sorrow sad;
The heart in which a little love may creep
          Is not all bad.

THE WAY OF THE WORLD.

SINCE Adam's first sin in the garden of song,
　Where the hopes of the race were empearled,
Whenever a mortal does anything wrong,
　It is only the way of the world!

If statesmen forget all the pledges they made,
　And the people to evils are hurled,—
Excuse their misdeeds!　'Tis a trick of the trade,
　And is only the way of the world!

If bankers, confusing distinctions of wealth,
　Have your gold to their own pockets whirled,
And then gone to Europe for pleasure and health—
　It is only the way of the world.

If preachers, forgetting the Master of old
　And the banner of light He unfurled,
Elope with the fairest ewe-lambs of the fold,—
　It is only the way of the world.

If merchants, unscrupulous, cheat with a will
　While their lips are at honesty curled,—
Harsh blame, hie away! And your censure, be still!
　It is only the way of the world!

The way of the world!   What a happy excuse
For the faults and the follies unfurled!
Bind virtue securely!   The vices turn loose!
'Tis the way—'tis the way—of the world!

MY SHADOW AND I.

A SOMETHING, not of earth or sky,
  Beside me walks the ways I go,
  And I—I never truly know,
If I am it or it is I.

It soothes me with its tender speech,
  It guides me with its gentle hand,
  But I—I can not understand
The links that bind us each to each.

I hear the songs of golden days
  Fall softly on the saddened years,
  But know not whose the hungry ears
First feasted on the roundelays.

I feel the hopes, the yearnings brave,
  Within my bosom surge and roll,
  But know not whose the Master Soul
That called their glories from the grave.

I see the great world's greater curse,
   Dark struggles on through darker days,
   But know not whose the eyes that gaze
Through all the sobbing universe.

O, Shadow mine! Beneath my brow
   I feel thy thoughts, and in my heart
   Thy fondest longings madly start!
Thou art myself and I am thou!

IN THE VALES.

WHEN from these vales I go,
   That slumber on in dreams,
     O, will the summer winds dance to and fro,
  And kiss the streams
That play where roses scatter fond perfume
And lilies burst with bloom ?

Glad children of the spring,
  They moan their music sweet
Where tangled grasses wave, and softly sing
  Where meadows meet,
And wildwood shadows drooping bless
The groves with happiness.

Their soothing songs I hear
  Among the granite hills,
Above the elfin warbles rich and clear
  From rippling rills,
As if they called my soul in future days
To wander all their ways.

Ah, moaning winds, you seem
  To fill my musing breast
With lullabies that linger as I dream
  And bring me rest;
For melodies from your low voices creep
That soothe my heart with sleep!

THE WILLOW.

A SONG for the willow, the wild weeping willow,
  That murmurs a dirge to the rapturous days,
  And moans when the kiss of the breeze laden
    billow
Entangles and dangles among the sad sprays!
A musical ditty to scatter the sadness,
  A warble of wildness to banish its tears,
Till tremulous measures of bountiful gladness
  Be sounding and bounding through all of the
    years.

The beautiful brooks,as they waken from slumbers,
  Pause under the shadows that fall from the
  boughs,
And weave their caresses in passionate numbers,
  While soothing and smoothing the frowns from
  its brows;
But chained in the desolate sorrows of weeping
  Its heart never warms to the raptures of mirth,
And over its bosom no pleasures are creeping
  While wending and blending their joys with the
  earth.

Then sing for the willow, the wild weeping willow,
  That droops in the smiles of the summer-born
  times,
And mourns in the kiss of the sweet-scented billow,
  When beaming and gleaming are dripping with
  chimes!
While melodies move where their happiness lingers,
  They surely will gladden the tear-laden sprays,
And music that flutters from fairy-like fingers
  Will lighten and brighten the burdensome days.

AT THE MILL.

THE water-wheel goes 'round and 'round
  With heavy sighs of mournful sound,
  While dismal cries and weary moans
Unite with sad and tearful groans,
And weeping waves of water throw
  Afar the echoes of their sadness,
And cadences of plaintive woe
  Dispel each little note of gladness.

My daily life goes 'round and 'round,
And rest for me is never found;
The sobbing dirges of distress
Are more than songs of happiness;
The shadows of despairing doom
  Condemn to-day and curse to-morrow,
And muffled terrors fill the gloom
  Which offers anguish to my sorrow.

But hope, O, heart, for future weal!
The waters rest beyond the wheel;
So life may sing when toil is done
And all its battles lost or won.
There lives a sweeter music there,
  Of gentle and melodious measure,
Where weeping never comes and where
  The ages perish into pleasure.

SHADOW AND SHINE.

THEY will find in this life who are grieved with
 its gladness
 No songs for the heart and no hopes for the soul,
But will faint in the glooms where the dirges of
 sadness
 In tremulous murmurs of wretchedness roll ;
For the sweets of this earth never lavish their kisses
 Where lives in the valleys of rapture repine ;
In the tortures they mourn who denounce all the
 blisses,—
 They weep in the shadow that rail at the shine.

In the fields that are fair with the blooms of the
 clover,
 No garlands are grown for the arbors of shade
Where the woes of the wood in their darkness hang
 over
 The grasses that wave with the winds of the
 glade ;
From the chimes of the breezes there echo no
 measures
 That gladden the gale with a music divine ;
In the troubles they languish who shrink from the
 pleasures,
 They weep in the shadow that rail at the shine.

Ah, the world is abounding with wonderful glories
　And wild are the warbles that sweeten its ways
While the songs of the land sing their beautiful
　　stories,
　And scatter their melodies over the days !
There are smiles, there are joys, never mingled with
　　sorrow,
　O, man, in return for the tears that are thine,
And the soul never sobs that has hopes for the
　　morrow,
　Nor weeps in the shadow nor rails at the shine !

THE GROWTH OF SONG.

A TENDER song in shadows grew,
　　And humble hearts were homes it knew.

But through its wondrous music stole
The longings of the human soul ;

The hopes of hosts unsatisfied
Within its numbers wandered wide ;

And strangely wet with toilsome tears
It held the yearnings of the years ;

Till millions with their woes oppressed,
Proclaimed the song of peace and rest ;

Till nations in their troubled ways
Found comfort in the joyous lays,

And all the halting race of wrong
Exalts the loving might of song !

Ah, song that soothes our many cries
With fondness of thy lullabies,

We love, we bless, we scepter thee
Proud empress of the hearts that be !

SPRING AND MUSIC.

SPRING, among her sylvan shades,
  And the gladness of her glades,
    Once in dreamy hours was straying,
Where sweet Music with her throngs
Of glad melodies and songs
  In the happy vales was playing.

Pan beheld the fairy maids
As they gamboled in the shades,
  And he swore they should not sever,
But that o'er the blooming land,
Heart to heart and hand in hand,
  They should wander on forever.

Thus when come the gentle days
O'er the wildwood's tangled ways,
   There is found no gloomy weather ;
For among the leafy bowers
And the valleys bright with flowers
   Spring and Music walk together !

COMPENSATION.

THE softest beams of the stars are born in the
      farthest skies,
   And fairest rays of the sun where evening
      shadows rise ;
The sweetest songs of the bird are sung in the
   darkest days,
And rarest blooms of the spring are found in the
   wildest ways.

The brightest blush of the rose is blown as the
   petals fade.
The greenest grass of the earth is grown in the
   hidden glade ;
The fondest rhyme of the rill is heard in the secret
   vale,
And lightest lays of the breeze are borne from the
   dying gale. .

The highest hopes of the heart in saddest of sorrows
grow,
The purest pleasures of joy arise in the wane of
woe ;
The gladdest smiles of the lips are seen in the hours
of pain,
And proudest days of the free are spent by the
broken chain.

The grandest deeds of the race are writ on the
faded scroll,
The truest rivers of good from villainous fountains
roll ;
The perfect raptures of life are reared in the arms
of care,
And Hope with her joys dispels the darkness of our
despair.

MY MOLLIE, O !

'TWAS in the summer's sweet perfume,
   When roses bloomed and holly, O,
That in the brightness of her bloom,
   I first did meet my Mollie, O.

Although she said for lives to love
   Was nothing but pure folly, O,
My heart was lit with light above,
   And I true loved my Mollie, O.

O, swift and fast the days did flee
   And seemed most bright and jolly, O,
For evermore was near to me
   My fair and lovely Mollie, O.

Now I doth sit through all the day
   And nurse my melancholy, O,
For from me she has turned away,
   O, false and fickle Mollie, O !

SING NOT OF BEAUTY.

SING not of beauty's grace to me ;
    Its very name a story tells
Of doubly dark inconstancy,
    Love falser than a hundred hells.

Its face is often but a screen
    To hide a devil's heart of guile,
Of thoughts and deeds of shameful mien,
    By winning looks of heartless wile.

Its laughing smile is but the gleam
    That springs from dross of foulest make ;
It stirs a sweet but idle dream,
    Then leaves the trusting heart to break.

Sing not of beauty's grace to me ;
    I can not bear to hear the name ;
For, oh ! Too oft in it I see
    A soul of falsehood and of shame !

AT EVENTIDE.

AT eventide, when glories lie
 In crimson curtains hung on high,
  And all the breast of heaven glows
With mingled wreaths of flowers and snows,
The dearest dreams of life draw nigh.

The pleasures in their soft robes fly
With angel wings adown the sky,
 And rapture lulls to sweet repose,
  At eventide.

Ah, well-a-day! Life's weary cry,
And all its curse and care shall die,
 When Age on downy couches throws
 His weary limbs and only knows
The tender dreams of bye-and-bye,
  At eventide !

WHEN CHRISTMAS COMES.

WHEN Christmas comes, what pleasures
      spring
  From drooping hearts on happy wing,
    Like joyous birds that soaring rise
    From hidden coverts to the skies,
And echo in the chimes that ring !

Glad millions in wild rapture sing
Hosannaed hopes of welcoming,
    While praises blend in harmonies,
      When Christmas comes.

Ah, happy hours ! Around them cling
The dearest joys that life may bring,
    And all the world's despairing cries
    Are soothed to sleep with lullabies
That banish every bitter thing,
      When Christmas comes !

WHEN THOU ART NEAR.

WHEN thou art near, with gladdest grace
My heart is held in fond embrace,
For laughing lips with raptures bless
The toils and tears of my distress,
And woes within me have no place.

The halting hours with hurried pace
Whirl wildly on through happy space,
And life is light with happiness,
When thou art near.

Like mortals whom an angel race
Renews with gladness face to face,
I thrill with Love's unseen caress
That holy hands upon me press,
And Heaven's pleasures all I trace,
When thou art near.

HE SLEEPS AT LAST.

HE sleeps at last! The vales of rest
   Are waiting for the war-worn breast,
      And glorious angels fondly spread
   The sweetest roses for his bed,
While countless millions call him blest.

Fame welcomes him with glad behest,
While garlands on his brow are pressed,
   And laurels cluster o'er his head;
      He sleeps at last.

O, deep the sorrows here confessed,
Where Freedom makes eternal quest!
   The wondrous chief that proudly led
   The long, blue lines that fought and bled,
In peace is now no more distressed;
      He sleeps at last!

WHEN FORTUNES FROWN.

WHEN fortunes frown, the woes, bedight
   With brooding shadows, bring the night,
      While dismal sorrows darkness dole,
      And disappointments rise and roll
Above the longings for the- light.

Despair, with hands that curse and blight,
Sows weakness in the hearts of might
   Until they falter near the goal,
      When fortunes frown.

But onward still!   The valleys white
With Heaven's blossoms are in sight;
   The Holy Mountains, knoll on knoll,   .
   Are waiting for the Master Soul,
And he shall conquer for the right,
      When fortunes frown!

WHEN WE SHALL MEET.

WHEN we shall meet, I strangely know
  The mad emotions that shall flow
  Across my heart all quivering,
 Beneath the raptures he shall bring
From angel years that gladdened so.

And I all shy and silent grow
Beneath his glance of gladness, though
  Wild yearnings through my bosom spring,
  When we shall meet.

Till joyful tears of passion show,
And to his kind embrace I throw
  My heart unworthy, and I cling
  With deathless fondness to the king
I worshipped in the Long Ago,
  When we shall meet!

SWEET EYES OF BLUE.

SWEET eyes of blue! The stars by night,
  That swoon the world with laughing light,
  And touch the hills with tender glow
  While all the vales are kissed below,
Beside you would no more be bright.

My worlds ye are, and while I throw
My heart to catch the beams that flow
  From your fair shrine, my woes take flight,
    Sweet eyes of blue!

Glad orbs of beauty! In your sight
My soul mounts up with secret might,
  Till Eden's lovely bowers I know;
  And as through Heaven's gates I go,
The pleasures all my sorrow smite,
    Sweet eyes of blue!

HAD WE NOT MET.

HAD we not met, the brooding woe
   And all the griefs that greater grow,
      Might not have been, and happy-wise
   Our lives have laughed with lullabies
And quaffed such joys as few may know.

Our days beneath embittered skies
Where anguish moans and sorrow cries,
   Might not have wept and wandered so,
      Had we not met!

But ah, my darling!   All we prize,—
Love and sweet trust that never dies,
   Wild yearnings that with constant flow
   From kindred heart to bosom go,—
Would never in our souls had rise,
      Had we not met!

A SONNET.

WE gentler grow by sorrow; not the breast
    That never crouches in the nights of tears,
    That never bends beneath the loads of years,
Has sympathies that are the kindliest.
There is a strength in agony that best
    Can link the careless heart with human fears,
    And teach it that fond kindness which endears
The millions that with sadness are oppressed.

Grief softens while it saddens; pleasure smites
    The timid soul with harshness, till it knows
    Small earnest of the great world's grievous woes
And little of its struggles; sorrow plights
Her troth with sorrow, and in tears unites
    Man unto man and hatred overthrows.

OKLAHOMA,— A SONNET.

HERE, through the ages old, the desert slept
  In solitudes unbroken, save when passed
  The bison herds, and savage hunters swept
In thund'ring chaos down the valleys vast;
But, lo! Across the barren margins stepped
  Advancement with her legions, and one blast
  From her imperial trumpet filled the last
Lone covert where affrighted wildness crept.

Full armed, full armored, at her wondrous birth,
  Her shining temples wreathed with gorgeous
    dower,
She sits among the empires of the earth;
  Her proud achievements o'er the nations tower,
Won by her people with their royal worth,
  With lofty culture, wisdom, wealth and power.

ESTRANGED

THOUGH far apart, my darling, side by side
   We wander still and our fond yearnings meet,
   As when our hearts with highest raptures beat
Before our footsteps trod the paths of pride;
Our close companionship hath never died;
   True love and trust are always fair and sweet,
And time from life's best hopes can never hide
   A kindred soul that made its own complete!
So thou, dear one, shalt come once more to me,
   The sweeter grown for all thy years of pain;
My longing arms shall open wide for thee,
   And thou shalt nestle on my breast again;
Then perfect love shall richly crown the years,
And both be better for our griefs and tears.

RECONCILED.

WE meet again beyond the barren past,
    Beyond the pride, the sorrows and the tears;
    And yearnings leave the strife and hate of
    years
To flood our souls with perfect peace at last!
Our hearts forget the wrong so deep and vast,
    The wounding words and all the cruel woe,
    Till joy is all our bounding bosoms know,
And life is glad with happiness at last.

Love, deathless and forgiving, crowns with bays
    The future and our hopes, as full of grace,
As youth had fondly dreamed in other days,
    When first we knew how sweet was her embrace.
God's endless purpose guides the feet of men;
Beyond our pride we meet in love again!

THE DYING HERO.

HIS greatness hath not left him; till the years
    Have won the nation from her children dead,
    And robbed her of remembrance where she
    rears
Her monuments above the blood they shed,
Will his name want for homage; with sad fears
    The Union winds her garlands o'er his head,
And fondly wreathes her love, bedewed with tears,
    To bless the hero on his dying bed.

His luster lives untarnished; as he lies
    Where Malady has bound him in wild pain,
And only Death can loose the heavy chain
    That galls her captive while his nature dies,
He seems far greater in his country's eyes,
    Than if an Appomattox spake again.

SONNET.

SOMEHOW, someway, I can not see the light;
  The giant hills of doubting reach the skies,
    Abiding shadows bring eternal night,
And on my ways no suns of morning rise;
Dark mysteries across the years of might
  Crush down my hopes, until each yearning dies,
Until my soul is weary, dim my sight,
  And ghostly echoes mock my fainting cries.

Ah, I shall know beyond these narrow years,
  The glorious mornings of eternal day,
  Where perfect love and tender trust shall play,
And smiles and laughter banish all the tears,
And all the heavy mists of doubts and fears
  Shall leave my longing soul somehow, someway !

GREATNESS LIVES APART.

GREAT natures live apart ; the mountain gray
     May call no comrade to his lonely side;
  The giant ocean, wrapped in storm and spray,
  Has no companion for her endless tide ;
  The forest monarch, where his parents died,
Can find no brother in his lofty sway,
     And mighty rivers chafe their margins wide
Where infant rills and childish fountains play.

So heroes live ; no raptured blossoms start
     Where rugged heights of human glory end ;
     No tender songs of loving beauty blend
Their chorus in the great man's peerless heart ;
Fate fills their souls with magnitude, and art
     Supplies their lives with no congenial friend.

POEMS.

POEMS are holy things. Eternal Truth,
    Borrowing the robes of song and lovely grown,
    In them her glory unto man proclaims
And fills his longing soul. They softly speak
Of Nature's beauty and the secrets old
Concealed behind the shadows of the hills,
And love on angel fingers borne to men,
Naming them over in so sweet a voice
That music leads their footsteps in the ways
Where God has walked ; and with a lofty Harp,
As wondrous as the gentle harps of heaven,
Uplifts, ennobles, soothes and leads the race
Unto its last great ultimate of power,
To words of tenderness and goodly deeds.

SINGER AND SONG.

A SINGER sang in sorrow long
    And breathed his life into his song.

Unknown, unheard, the song went wide,
Until the singer, starving, died.

Now in their hearts the nations write
And wear the singer's song of might.

Ah, singers fail and fall from view,
But songs are always, always new !

If garlands none to singers cling,
Bays wreathe above the songs they sing.

TO ONE WHO PLEDGED HER FRIEND-
SHIP.

WITHIN this false world we may count our-
selves blest,
    If we have but one friend who is faithful and
      true ;
And so in your friendship contented I'll rest,
    And believe I have found that one blessing in you.

THE BANKS O' TURKEY RUN.

LIKE a thousan' birds o' brightness from the isles
    o' summer seas,
    Rickollections, full o' gladness, come with songs
      and lullabies,
An' I listen to the carols that with gentle voices
    roll,
Full o' tenderness an' beauty, down upon my weary
    soul,
Fer thar's one thet keeps a-singin' with a song thet's
    never done,
An' I see the bendin' willers on the banks o' Turkey
    Run.

An' agin' I be a youngster with a youngster's foolin'
   dreams,
With his high-falutin' notions an' his fiddle-faddle
   schemes ;
With the laughin' an' the cryin', with the sorrow an'
   · the joy,
Thet is jumbled up together in the bosom o' the
   boy;
An' agin my arly fancies in a fairy loom are spun
Underneath the dancin' shadders on the banks o'
   Turkey Run.

An' agin I be a school-boy with the other merry
   lads,
When Joe an' Jerry, Bill an' I, wus only little tads,
When a half a dozen marvels an' a kivered ball was
   worth—
With a knife o' Barlow pattern—all the treasures o'
   the earth ;
An' the soundin' sort o' thunder from a poppin'
   kind o' gun
Set our faces all a-giggle on the banks o' Turkey
   Run.

It 'ud tickle any feller but ter see the solemn
   look,
When the master was a-watchin', thet we fastened
   on the book,

But the mischief stickin' in us, like pertaters in a
    sack,
It wus never hard ter empty when the teacher
    turned his back ;
O, the paper wads we tumbled thet 'ud weigh about
    a ton,
In thet crazy-cornered school-house on the banks o'
    Turkey Run !

How we used ter chase the robins an' the rabbits
    in the wood,
How we gethered bloomin' posies in the sighin'
    solitude !
How we wundered all the medders in our roamin's
    o'er an' o'er,
How we teetered in the branches o' the beech an'
    sycamore !
Or we watched the rompin' minners as they
    rasseled in their fun,
While we nearly bust a-laughin', on the banks o'
    Turkey Run !

How we used ter go a-fishin' when the day wus
    gittin' late,
With a little line o' cotton an' a fish-worm fer a
    bait !
With a bent pin for a fish-hook an' a hazel fer a
    pole,
How we sought the softest places by the widest,
    deepest hole !

How we teehee-eed at the nibbles, caught the fishes
    one by one,
With the biggest kind o' prowess, on the banks o'
    Turkey Run !

When the sun was burnin' shavin's in the heatin'
    stove o' June,
An' the clock upon the mantle wus a-knockin' off
    the noon ;
When the beams in bunches blistered as they never
    did afore,
An' the sweat was drippin', droppin', from the
    mouth o' every pore,
How we skipped across the medder, how our
    swimmin' wus begun,
In the cool an' crystal waters 'tween the banks o'
    Turkey Run !

O, the smilin' days o' childhood !   O, the loudly
    laughin' years !
When contentment brings the moments neither
    heaviness ner tears !
When the pleasures jine the longin's an' the fairy
    fingers roll
All the heaps o' angel music in upon the blazin'
    soul !
O, my Joe an' Bill an' Jerry !   Trustin' comrades,
    you wus won
Whar my bare feet brushed the grasses on the banks
    o' Turkey Run !

But, alas ! Thar wus another ; she was fairer than
the rest,
An' she allus had a hearin' fer the wishes o' my
breast ;
Allus wus a chunk o' sunshine an' a piece o' quiet
glee,
Allus had a smile o' welcome an' a tender word
fer me ;
An' without her wus no shinin' an' o' happiness wus
none
Ter bring gladness ter my bosom on the banks o'
Turkey Run.

O, her home wus in a cottage whar the mornin'-
glories hung,
An' the arly birds o' April with their sweetest music
sung ;
Thar wus roses 'round her winder, thar wus roses
'round her door,
Thet wus stickin' full o' blushes, but they allus
blushed the more,
When her eyes wus seen a-peepin' an' her cheeks
beamed like the sun,
From thet cosy little cottage on the banks o'
Turkey Run !

Many an' many a time we wundered in the grassy
medder-land
With our wishes right together an' our longin's
hand in hand ;

How we dreamed about the future when the world
    should give me fame,
An' when she would be thrice noble to be worthy o'
    my name !
Thus we talked an' thus we fancied ; others might
    my boyhood shun,
But I found her kind, my sweetheart, on the banks
    o' Turkey Run.

But the times have been a-changin' sence them arly
    years o' joy,
When she wus but a little girl an' I a little boy ;
When Joe an' Jerry, Bill an' I, together wus at play,
With our hearts as light as feathers, every minute
    of the day,
An' at twilight sunk ter slumber tell the mornin'
    wus begun,
In the gloomy silent forests on the banks o' Turkey
    Run.

Bill an' Joe have gone a-rovin' on a fortune-huntin'
    quest
Through the silver mines an' Injuns in the moun-
    tains o' the west ;
But the janders came ter Jerry with a solemn sort
    o' call
Tell they painted him as yaller as a punkin in the
    fall ;

An' to-day I saw his tombstone as it glittered in the
sun,
Over in the little churchyard, on the banks o'
Turkey Run !

An' alas, my precious sweetheart !   Like a lily,
virgin white,
Did she slowly fade an' wither tell her spirit took
its flight !
Like an angel into heaven did she sweetly, calmly
creep,
An' her lovely life wus over an' her bosom went ter
sleep ;
An' the tollin', tollin' church-bells dropt the dirges
one by one,
As we laid her 'neath the willer on the banks o'
Turkey Run.

Thar a little cross o' marble marks the sacred,
silent shade,
Whar the fair an' laughin' beauty o' my ole sweet-
heart wus laid ;
An' the summer has a sadness thet is cryin' through
the years,
An' my heart is full o' sorrow, an' mine eyes is full
o' tears,
Fer I've allus had a failin', sence her friendship first
I won,
Fer thet little lovin' maiden on the banks o'
Turkey Run !

But them days have past forever in the years o'
    long ago,
An' a wishin' ter be wealthy has enraptured Bill an'
    Joe ;
Death has taken Jerry ; only I, o' all the boys,
Am' remainin' ter remember all them arly angel
    joys ;
But to-night I see their faces as they peep in full o'
    fun,
An' agin we're boys together, on the banks o'
    Turkey Run !

www.ingramcontent.com/pod-product-compliance
Lightning Source LLC
Chambersburg PA
CBHW031157050726
47495CB00019B/2447